I am NOT CONTAGIOUS

Angela K. Pearson

I Am Not Contagious

by Angela K. Pearson
www.angelapearson.com

Copyright © 2020

All Rights Reserved

No portion of this book may be reproduced in any form or by any means (which includes mechanically, electronically, or by any other means, including photocopying), without written permission from the author. Permission should be addressed in writing to
angela@angelapearson.com

Disclaimer

This book contains the ideas and opinions of its author. The intention of this book is to provide information, helpful content, and motivation to readers about the subjects addressed for children and their parents. It is published and sold with the understanding that the author is not engaged to render any type of psychological, medical, legal, or any other kind of personal or professional advice. All references to historical events, real people, or real places are used fictitiously. Other names, characters, places, and events are products of the author's imagination, and any resemblances to actual events or places or persons, living or dead, is entirely coincidental. No warranties or guarantees are expressed or implied by the author's choice to include any of the content in this volume. The author shall not be liable for any physical, psychological, emotional, financial, or commercial damages, including, but not limited to, special, incidental, consequential, or other damages. The reader is responsible for their own choices, actions, and results.

1st Edition. 1st printing 2021

Interior Design by Steve Walters at Oxygen Publishing Inc.

Independently Published by Oxygen Publishing Inc.
397 Main Road,
Hudson, QC, Canada J0P 1P0
www.oxygenpublishing.com

ISBN: 978 1 0879 5035 8
Imprint: Independently published

DEDICATION

I dedicate this book to the loves of my life; my children Darren, Keyara, and Grayson. Thank you for giving me courage and purpose. I will always stand up for you and for what is right. To my grandchildren, I pave this path for you.

It is with sincere gratitude that I dedicate this book to those who have fought and continue to fight on the front lines for medical freedom. My heart goes out to those who have suffered, and who are suffering. You are not just freedom warriors, you are brave hearts.

This book will forever serve in memory of you.

~

I give sincere thanks to God for giving me strength and guidance during this process. With Him, all things are possible.

Hi, my name is Grayson, I'm six and I'm just like most kids my age. I love school and I really like learning about the anatomy of sharks and the human body. I think robotics engineering is the coolest and someday I'm going to build a robot that will help many people in some way.

How do you think robots can help people?

I have been going to school all my life but this particular year was such a big deal because I was officially a 1st grader. No more preschool and no more kindergarten. This was the start of being a big kid. I could feel it in my bones. My mom was super proud. She even took a picture.

Even though I couldn't wait to meet my new teacher and make new friends, I may have been a teeny tiny bit afraid to walk into the school by myself. Everyone gets afraid sometimes!

My mom walked with me as far as she was allowed and after meeting my teacher, I realized there was no real reason for me to be afraid. She was super nice and I made some pretty awesome friends.

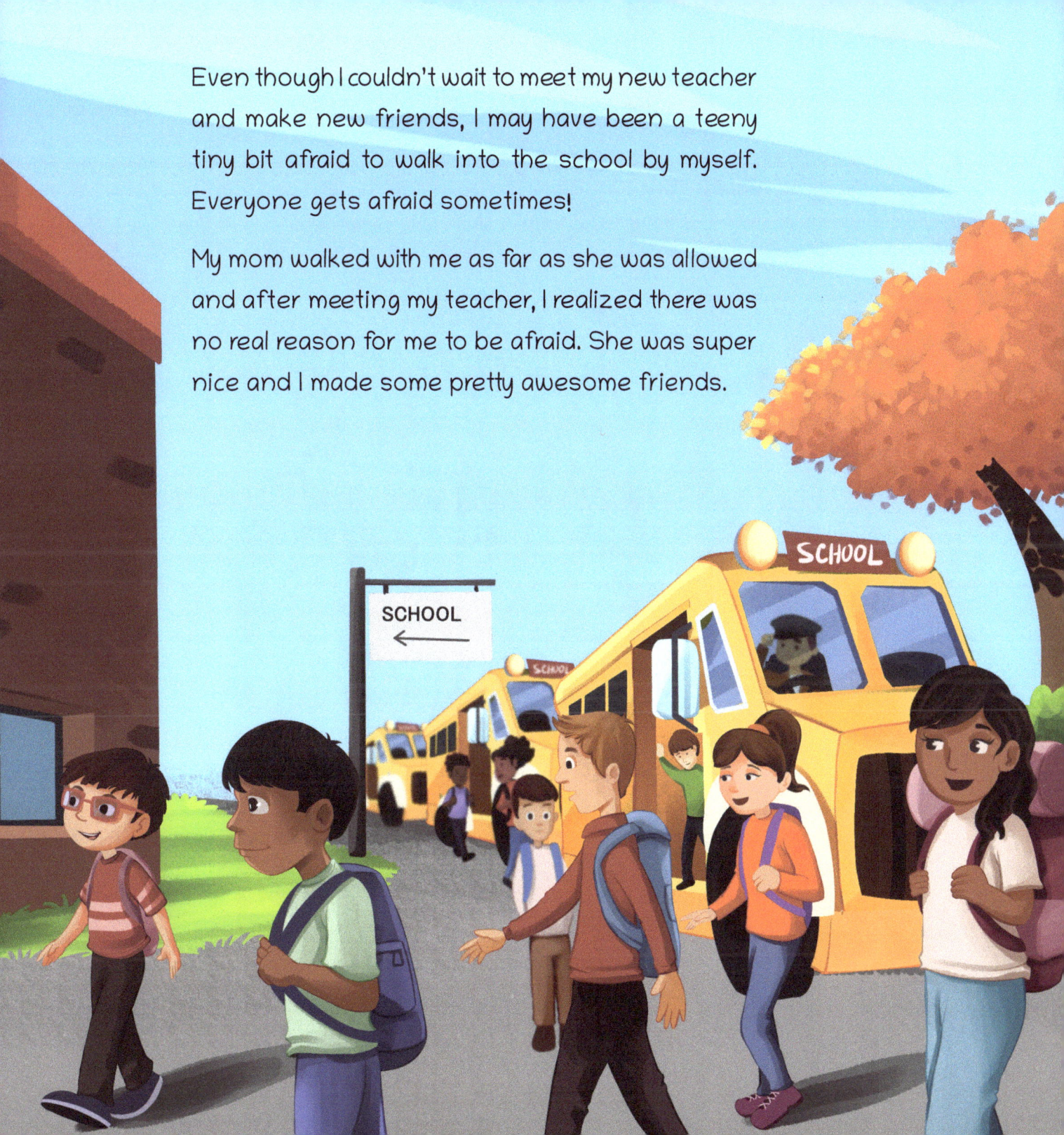

Then all of a sudden this happened. Yup, that's the New York state governor and he kicked me and every other healthy kid out of school. I thought everyone was allowed to go to school. The governor of our state said, "No shots, no school." I didn't understand at first but then my mom explained this new rule.

She called it tyranny!

I had 14 days to say goodbye to my friends and my teacher. On my last day of school, my mom wanted to make it special so she sent a basket full of treats to share with my whole class.

Everyone took turns giving me hugs. Even though I was sad, I know things happen for a reason and it's important we learn from whatever happens to us so we can help others who may not understand.

But I'm sure going to miss them!

So, what are shots? They are vaccinations that many of us kids typically get, starting when we are just babies. Some say they protect us against certain germs. My mom says these shots may not be the healthiest for me just as peanut butter may not be the healthiest for some kids.

Some people think that my mom should not have a choice to not give me shots.

Some grown-ups are afraid of me because I don't get shots. They think I am contagious like I have a disease or something. That's so silly! I am not contagious, I am not sick. I cannot give you something I do not have. Some even say, I shouldn't go to the same school as their kids.

It's okay. Their words may hurt my feelings but I am not mad at them. They are just nervous about what they do not know.

Phlegmy Wimble is a not so nice talk show host on T.V. He is a big bully. He talks way too much and makes a lot of mean jokes about parents who don't give their kids shots.

If I were ever on his show, I would teach him a thing or two, starting with giving him a tissue. YUCK!

Next, I would show him how to be kind by showing him compassion for his lack of empathy.

Having compassion for others is a special super power. Phlegmy Wimble is one of few people who do not have this.

Okay, I'm afraid of the dark SOMETIMES because I can't see anything. I know there's nothing there but I'm just a kid and my imagination can play tricks on me.

My night light helps me a little but I still can't see everything. If we only keep a small light on, how will we ever see the whole picture?

When I flip the light on, I can see everything. We have to turn the light on inside our head too and we'll see that there is no such thing as the boogeyman.

Headlight! Haha get it?

My friend Jasiah gets shots.

I know his mom loves him just like my mom loves me.

Good parents want to protect their kids no matter what.

My mom is protecting me; the way Jasiah's mom believes she is protecting him.

Shots or no shots!

Both our moms would never want anything to hurt us.

"Dear Governor Dodo,

I am taught to use my voice.
Writing this speech is my very own choice;

I don't understand, not one little bit.
This makes no sense, not one little bit.

I can go to the zoo with Sarah and Drew,
We can swing on a swing, even sing if we please,
We can slide down a slide and ride on a ride,
I can flip at the gym with Darren and Tim,
We can school at the library, travel to Newbury
I can take Muay Thai, but I can't wear a school tie?

I don't understand, not one little bit.
This makes no sense, not one little bit.
I don't understand any of it."

Are you afraid?

I'm just in 1st grade. When I am afraid
I flip on the light and let it shine bright.

You kicked me out, I'm calling you out because
of you, yes it's true; your new rule is pretty cruel.

I don't understand, not one little bit.
This makes no sense, not one little bit.

I'm homeschooled now; don't dare take a bow,
My mom's resignation gets the standing ovation.

Your headlight's broken, so let's be open...
I can ride on a train, a bus and a plane,
I can dance at a party with Josh and Marty,
I can go to the mall with Keyara and Paul,
But I can't go to school with Sam and Jewel?

I don't understand, not one little bit. This makes no sense, not one little bit. I don't understand any of it.

I am NOT contagious, but rather courageous Your rule is outrageous and even OUTLANDISH.

… I understand what I just said and what I said makes sense in my head.

I understand every last bit. Now's not the time to throw a fit. This makes sense, every last little bit.

I am NOT contagious not the least little bit and kids like me don't deserve this. That's it."

Civic Ideals and Practices

Complete the crossword puzzle and acquire an understanding of your basic freedoms and citizen rights, and learn which practices support and protect them.

WORD BANK • Legislator • 1986 Act • Bill of Rights • Constitution • Government • Tyranny • Governor • Medical Freedom • Vaccination • VAERS •

Across

4. National Childhood Vaccine Injury Act that protects pharmaceutical companies from being sued for vaccine injuries.
5. Ratified in 1791 and guaranteeing such rights as the freedoms of speech, assembly, and worship.
6. An elected public official responsible for implementing state laws & overseeing the operation of the state executive branch.
7. The action or manner of controlling or regulating a nation, organization, or people.
10. A person who makes laws; a member of a legislative body

Down

1. A biological medical procedure with the intent to provide immunity to infectious diseases that carries risks of injury.
2. Provides important limitations on the government that protect the fundamental rights of United States citizens.
3. The right to refuse a medical procedure that carries risks of injury.
8. A form of government in which the ruler is an absolute dictator (not restricted by a constitution of laws or opposition).
9. Vaccine Adverse Event Reporting System, where vaccine reactions are reported.

For the solution and to download a FREE coloring book go to

www.angelapearson.com

Fun Word Search Challenge

Here's another great puzzle to work on. Locate all 21 words below in eight possible directions in the grid opposite! If you need more of a challenge give yourself a time limit of just 10 minutes!

HEALTHY	GOVERNOR	DREAM
SUPERHERO	GRATEFUL	HEADLIGHT
MANNERS	MOM	SHARE
COMPASSION	SCHOOL	VOICE
GRAYSON	RESEARCH	PROTECT
DAD	HUG	SUPERPOWER
FRIENDS	QUESTION	FREEDOM

For the solution and to download a FREE coloring book go to

www.angelapearson.com

```
U G Y D A D V L M Z Q M S D X O N K A Y
A I V O I C E N Z F U G R S Q W I M B T
D P G N L Z V O G R A T E F U L R P W A
E E F D G A T S O D Z O K T C E T O R P
S R O K G E O Y V Z C C V S C H O O L K
G Q A V X Y A A S R I W U K P D U L C S
H V J H D Y T R H W A C H T M S Y R R C
Z Z Q P S D E G Q J B Z M Q F M N G U H
I B N S K N R D T M A E A I H K F B C Q
D J Y Q N R V S U P E R H E R O S D Z V
U R Y A H C H M U M L B Y M R Y G R J G
F E M H L R E S E A R C H M O D E E R F
X W U B T A Q G C G O V E R N O R A M K
I O P B R L X N O I S S A P M O C M W F
U P T M D R A W I N Z B H E Z N R O H R
T R N O I T S E U Q H E A D L I G H T W
V E E I Z C S N H Z Y Q K O S Y U Q G S
F P J C U D L L I A Z T G T B W G G U P C
E U U Z O H S A K S D N E I R F M O M X
A S Z B Z B X W K G J J V Z X I P K L T
```

End of the book Discussion:

Do you think Grayson should be allowed to go to school?

Why or why not?

What do you think people can do differently?

How has Grayson's views inspired you?

How would you feel if you were Grayson?

Apparel

To order your **I am NOT contagious** apparel visit www.angelapearson.com

The Story Behind this Story

In June of 2019, Governor Andrew Cuomo of New York passed a new Bill into law removing religious exemptions that protected parents and their beliefs against vaccinations. This ultimately resulted in 26,000 children who could no longer exercise their basic right to access public or private education. My six-year-old son, Grayson, is one of those children.

After I left corporate America to take on the homeschooling life, Grayson had so many questions, that I felt compelled to share our story.

I wrote this book to influence change with the hope that we can feel compassion about issues we may not understand. It's more than just a book to me; it is written in my son's voice and the voices of every mother, father, and child fighting for medical freedom.

About the Author

Angela K. Pearson is passionate about her family. She is a devoted mother of three and enjoys helping her children discover their talents, whether that be wrestling, music, martial arts, a business goal or themselves. She considers her children to be her biggest accomplishment. Aside from their health and happiness, she makes it a priority that they understand their basic human rights and encourages them to lead their lives with a moral compass.

After her eldest son experienced an adverse reaction to a vaccine, she adopted a conservative approach to the sources from which she receives information.

Angela has been a holistic enthusiast for 20 years. She holds a Bachelor's degree in Behavioral Science and Community Health. She believes earning her degree is a bonus in her life, but it's not what defines her. She is strongly convinced that having a college education doesn't make a person smarter than a person without one and that education stems from being open to factual information that isn't indoctrinated or one-sided.

Being informed on vaccine ingredients and their direct effects, she opted out of the CDC's vaccine scheduled program. Her daughter and youngest son never received any vaccinations, and are perfectly healthy. Unfortunately, her eldest son was diagnosed with systemic lupus, the same autoimmune disease Angela's father had.

She advocates for informed consent regardless of where you stand on the matter and is confident that vaccines are not a one-size fits all. Given her history, she believes that every child should have their family history carefully examined along with the vaccine doses and ingredients before performing this type of medical procedure.

Angela is a lifestyle mentor and entrepreneur. **I Am Not Contagious** highlights not only her experience as a mother, her son's perspective, but also provides a systematic analysis of human behavior and how it relates to society and the lack of education on this topic.

To learn more about Angela K. Pearson you can visit www.angelapearson.com

CPSIA information can be obtained
at www.ICGtesting.com
Printed in the USA
JSHW051039150421
R10798600001B/R107986PG13507JSX00001B/1